THIS CANDLEWICK BOOK BELONGS TO:

_____

_____

_____

For Lauren, Allison, and Amanda, the best fish feeders in Texas
And for Sarah, in honor of her goldfish, Lucky

K. B.

For Diane

N. Z. J.

Text copyright © 2005 by Kelly Bennett
Illustrations copyright © 2005 by Noah Z. Jones

First paperback edition 2008

The Library of Congress has cataloged the hardcover edition as follows:

Bennett, Kelly.
Not Norman : a goldfish story / Kelly Bennett ; illustrated by Noah Z. Jones. —1st ed.
p. cm.
Summary: As a boy attempts to convince someone else to take his disappointing pet,
he learns to love Norman the goldfish himself.
ISBN 978-0-7636-2384-5 (hardcover)
[1. Pets—Fiction. 2. Goldfish—Fiction. 3. Friendship—Fiction.]
I. Jones, Noah Z., ill. II. Title
PZ7.B4425No 2005
[E]—dc22 2004051534

ISBN 978-0-7636-2763-8 (paperback)

15 16 17 18 19 TWP 19 18 17 16

Printed in Malaysia

This book was typeset in Shinn Medium.
The illustrations were created digitally.

Candlewick Press
99 Dover Street
Somerville, Massachusetts 02144

visit us at www.candlewick.com

NOT NORMAN

A Goldfish Story

Kelly Bennett

illustrated by **Noah Z. Jones**

CANDLEWICK PRESS

SESSION 1: BEFORE YOU READ

p. 1: Point to details in the illustrations to guide readers to look closely, and prompt them to say what they see.

"Look closely at the pictures. What do you notice? What could that be?"

Your Fish and You

When I got Norman, I didn't want to keep him.
I wanted a different kind of pet.

Not Norman.

I wanted a pet who could run and catch.
Or one who could climb trees and chase strings.
A soft, furry pet to sleep on my bed at night.
Not Norman.

All Norman does is swim around and around and around and around
and around and around and around and around. . . .

"This is it, Norman," I decide.
"I'm trading you for a good pet."
Norman doesn't move. Not even a fin twitches.

How can I trade him like this?
No one will want a sorry-looking fish in a gunky bowl.

When I drop Norman into his nice, clean bowl, he starts dipping and flipping, flapping his fins around. He looks so goofy I have to laugh.

"Don't think that just because you made me laugh, I'm going to keep you," I tell him. "Tomorrow, you're outta here."

Norman blows a stream of bubbles.

SESSION 1: AS YOU READ

pp. 6–9: Prompt children to check their predictions by retelling what's happened so far.

"Let's stop and retell what has happened so far. Does it match what you thought would happen?"

Not Norman, Gr. K Unit 4 Becoming Avid Readers Read-Aloud Reading Units of Study, © Calkins et al. 2015 (Heinemann).

The next day, I take Norman to school with me.
If I talk him up real good during Show-and-Tell,
maybe someone will want him.

On the way there, we see my friend Austin.
Austin has a real cool dog — and seven puppies.
"Wanna swap one of your pups for Norman?" I ask.
"Who's Norman?" asks Austin. "My goldfish," I say.

By the time I rescue Norman, half his water is gone!

"I'm sorry," I tell Norman when we get to school. "I'm really sorry."
He just stares at me all googly-eyed.

Finally it's my turn to Show-and-Tell.
Just as I start to talk about goldfish, Emily shouts,
"Jenny's gone! Who let my snake loose?"

Does anyone hear the story of how I got Norman?
Does anyone even ask to hold his bowl? No.
They're all jumping and screaming and chasing the snake.
Not Norman. He's looking right at me.

"Thanks for listening," I tell him.

That afternoon, we go to my music lesson.
As soon as it's over, I'm taking Norman back to the pet store.

I take out my tuba and begin to play.

Bom bom bo

I glance over at Norman. He's swaying back and forth.

Glu glu glu glug, he mouths.

"Look! Norman's singing," I say.

"Pay attention!" snaps Maestro. "And *try* to play the proper notes."

Baaaa Ba ba ba boooo Bo bo bo beeee.

Maestro makes me stay for extra practice.
By the time my lesson is over,
it's too late to go to the pet store.
"Don't think that just because you like my music,
I'm going to keep you," I tell Norman.

He glugs.

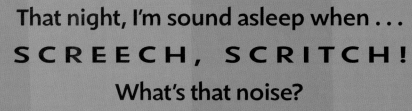

That night, I'm sound asleep when . . .
SCREECH, SCRITCH!
What's that noise?

SCRATCH SCRITCH SCREEEECH!

Yikes, there's something at the window!

Then, out of the corner of my eye,

I spot . . .

Norman!

He isn't scared.

He isn't swimming around in circles either.

He glugs and gives me a little wave.

I'm not alone.

Together, Norman and I slide open the curtains.
It was just a broken tree branch.

"Thanks for watching out for me, Norman."

On Saturday, I take Norman to the pet store, just like I said I would. I look at the cats and dogs and snakes and birds. I look at the hamsters and mice and lizards, too.

They all look like good pets,
but they are . . .

Not Norman.

When I got Norman, I wasn't sure I wanted to keep him.
But now, even if I could pick any pet
in the whole world, I wouldn't trade him.

Not Norman.

Kelly Bennett loves fish. "Fish are fun and funny," she says. "Just watching them makes me laugh." *Not Norman* is her first book with Candlewick Press. She is also the author of *Vampire Baby* and *Dad and Pop*, both illustrated by Paul Meisel. When she's not writing, Kelly creates tile mosaics and digs in her garden. She has two grown children and lives in Trinidad with her husband and their goldfish—whom she would never trade.

Noah Z. Jones loves drawing fish of all shapes and sizes, but especially smallish orange ones named Norman. In addition to *Not Norman*, he illustrated *The Monster in the Backpack* by Lisa Moser, *Welcome to the Bed and Biscuit* by Joan Carris, and *Those Shoes* by Maribeth Boelts. He lives in California.